Emily Huntington Miller

Captain Fritz

His Friends and Adventures

Emily Huntington Miller

Captain Fritz
His Friends and Adventures

ISBN/EAN: 9783744661225

Printed in Europe, USA, Canada, Australia, Japan

Cover: Foto ©Raphael Reischuk / pixelio.de

More available books at **www.hansebooks.com**

CAPTAIN FRITZ
His Friends and Adventures

BY

EMILY HUNTINGTON MILLER

Author of "What Tommy Did," "Royal Road to Fortune," etc.

NEW YORK

E. P. DUTTON & COMPANY

713 Broadway

1877

CONTENTS

CAPTAIN FRITZ:

HIS FRIENDS AND ADVENTURES.

CHAPTER I.

INTRODUCTION.

I AM the dog who lives at the Cemetery of St.
Angelo. Visitors always notice me as I sit at
the door of my house, and I hear them say, "What a
beautiful dog! He must be of a very great age!"

It is quite true. Since my mother died I am the very oldest dog in the world, and my friend the magpie has advised me to publish the story of my life. The magpie is a very wise bird. He has lived many years at the rectory of St. Angelo, and has a nest in the belfry of the church. He can also read and write, but that is a secret. He learned it from a sermon which he found one day lying upon a table. He carried it away to his nest and studied it for two years, so now he knows quite as much as the rector.

I am sure every one must remember the time when I was born, on account of a very remarkable circumstance. It was entirely dark for nine days. A very conceited young puppy once told me that the same thing happened when he was born, but this is a clear falsehood, for I was living at the time in the next street, and nothing of the sort took place. My friend the magpie has heard learned men at the rectory talking about this time, and he says there are even books written about it. It is called the Dark Ages. I was born, then, in the Dark Ages.

The first person with whom I became acquainted was my mother. She was very large and beautiful,

"LADY" AND HER CHILDREN.—Page 7.

and she was called Lady. A man who used to bring her a basin of bread and milk every morning called her so. My mother was very kind, and took excellent care of me, though there were three little dogs that were always getting in the way and made her a great deal of trouble. They were not at all like my mother. They had rough, woolly bodies, and short legs, with large, round feet, and were very ugly and disagreeable.

My mother was very proud of me, and began at once to train me; and when I was only two weeks old, the man who brought her breakfast took me up in his hand and said, "This little fellow is the pick of the lot. He will sell for a pretty penny. He must be taught to eat." From that time he began to teach me, also, and I soon learned to stand with my feet in the basin of cool milk and drink. The most convenient way to drink milk is to put your feet in the basin, but I have learned since then that it is not considered the proper thing in polite society.

One day, when the man fed us, a little boy came with him. He gave me something nice and sweet from his pocket, and then he carried me to another house, where a lady sat rocking a cradle. He put me in the lady's lap, and said:

"See, mamma, this is the little chap we shall sell to buy the baby some medicine. He is the very prettiest of them all."

The lady smiled a very little, and my mother came and laid her head on her knee. The baby's mother stroked her head softly, and said, "Poor Lady! I wonder if you care for your babies as I do for mine. I wonder if it breaks your heart to lose them!"

The thing they called a baby was very small and white. It had no hair, and it made a little weak noise, as if something hurt it.

The boy made a loud, strong noise when he talked and when he laughed. He squeezed me too tight in his hands, and he even put me in his pocket, and whistled to my mother to come home again.

After that the boy often took me out, but my mother always followed him and watched me every minute. It was much pleasanter in the house where the baby lived. Our house was called a barn and had no windows, but in the baby's house the sun shone, and there were swinging things in the windows, and baskets of round things that would roll about the floor when you upset them, and such delicious smells of meat and gravy. It seemed very dull to go back to the dark little corner, with only a few straws for playthings, and no company but those fat little dogs. But in a few weeks my adventures began.

CHAPTER II.

"WHO BUYS?"

ONE morning, before it was light, the boy came to bring us our breakfast, and while my mother was eating he took me in his arms and walked away. My mother followed a few steps, but he said, "No, no, Lady, you must stay at home; this little chap is going to see the world."

He shut the door of our house and I heard my mother crying inside, but the boy seemed to think it of no consequence.

"She'll forget all about you in a couple of days," he said, pulling my ears; "it would be very different now with my mother if the baby should go, but then, babies are of more consequence."

I should like to know why a little weak creature that cannot run or walk, or even bark, should be worth more than a dog with four feet that can run all day, and jump clear over his mother when she takes her nap on the straw. Even the magpie does not know that, but he says that when people say a thing for a great many years it becomes a fact. So this is a fact. Facts do not need to be explained.

The man and the boy took me to a place called a market. A great many people were coming and going, and the boy held me in his arms so that every one could see me. The man had radishes to sell and lettuce, and the people who bought often had dogs with them. The dogs always spoke to me, some of them very civilly, and one small brown dog offered to show me where there was something very delicious to eat; but the boy held me tight, and I could not get away. I should like to know what became of that brown dog. When the radishes were sold, the man took me up in his hand and began to offer me to the people, but most of them had their baskets filled, and went by very quickly, scarcely looking at me. The first who stopped was the butcher's boy. He had on a coat and a fine hat, but I knew it was the butcher's boy by his red eyes, and his hairy face, and his dreadful voice. He took me by the back of the neck, and held me up before his face, and I knew if my master turned his head, he would swallow me in a minute, for my mother told me so, when he once looked into the door of our house and frightened her into spasms. He said, "How much do you want for this little whiffet?"

"Ten dollars, if the gentleman pleases," said my master, very politely.

"Ten dollars! you must be joking. Why, I could have my pick of twenty grown dogs for five."

"But the gentleman sees this is no common dog. This is a French poodle—a performing dog; he can be taught all manner of tricks."

"What do I want of a performing dog? I want a dog to keep the rats out of my cellar and the mice out of my flour."

He gave me a little shake and tossed me back to my master. I curled down as close as I could, and fairly trembled with fright.

The next that stopped was a little girl. She had a sweet voice and a sweet face—the very sweetest face in the world. Her name was Elsie. She was singing when she came along, making a little noise just to herself, and when she saw me she said,

"Oh, the lovely little dog! May I see him—may I take him in my arms?"

My master put me in her arms, and she patted me and hugged me. Her coat was very soft, much softer than my master's or the boy's, and when she talked to me I forgot all about my mother and the little dogs and our house.

"Will the little lady buy the pretty dog?" asked my master.

"Oh, will you sell him? I wonder if grandmother would buy him. I suppose he is worth a great deal of money!"

"Only ten dollars. That is very little for such a dog."

The grandmother came along presently. Her

voice was very pleasant, and when she took me in her hands it was like being on a cushion or in the baby's cradle.

But she shook her head when she heard what I was worth. "Ten dollars for a mischievous little puppy! It was not to be thought of!"

"But madame sees this is a most valuable dog— a performing dog; he can be taught to do every-thing—almost to talk. His mother is celebrated. Madame must have heard of Lady, the dog who astonished every one with her tricks, and was so unfortunate as to lame her shoulder while exhibiting in Paris. This is one of Lady's puppies—the very pick of the lot. He would be worth his weight in gold if he were trained."

Madame only made a funny little noise, and shook her head, but not so much as before.

"Buy him for my birthday, Grandmother," said Elsie. "You said I might choose, and I choose this lovely little dog."

"And the party, and the ring, and the locket, and the silk dress! Will you have this little good-for-nothing rather than any of them?"

"Yes," said Elsie, "I choose the dog;" and she snatched me up in her arms and danced away, but came back in a minute to say to the boy,

"Is it your pet? Will you be very sorry to have it sold?"

"Oh, no, I shall be very glad," said the boy. "The money is to buy medicine for the baby. The baby is sick, and babies are worth much more than dogs."

"That is true, I suppose," said Elsie; and her grandmother nodded at the boy as if she thought him very wise, and said:

"Since the money is for the sick baby I do not so much mind paying it;" and then they went away.

Elsie held me in her arms, and promised me a great many beautiful things as we went along, but the grandmother paid no attention to either of us, only she smiled a little when Elsie said:

"I have named my dear little doggie, Grand- mother. I have called him Felix. Felix means for- tunate and happy."

CHAPTER III.

A NEW HOME.

O now I was Felix the Fortunate. To begin with, it was very grand to have a name of my own, and then if you could have seen my house! The one where the baby lived was nothing at all to it; I think you could almost have put it in one of the rooms. There was a very large yard for me to play in, all covered with green grass, except in some places where there were beautiful flowers. Flowers are not good to eat, and they make you sneeze when you smell of them, but the ground where they grow is very soft and nice to dig in, and it is great fun to make deep holes in it, and bury bones until they are tender and delicious.

There was a fountain in the yard; not a large fountain like the one here at St. Angelo, where it always rains, but a small one, with a man standing in the middle who spilled the water out of a pitcher set upon his head. Sometimes the pitcher was empty; then, of course, the water did not spill out. The first room into which Elsie carried me was very long, and had flowers all over the floor and steps leading up into the sky. There were pictures hanging in rooms all along the sides. I had never seen any pictures, and I thought these were people. They all looked at me, and when Elsie put me down, I was afraid. Then she opened another door, and said, "Come, Felix!"

I did not come. I did not know how. So she carried me again in her arms. This room was even better than the other. It had cushions and soft rugs lying about on the floor, and there was a fire burning in the grate. The best thing in the world is to lie on a soft rug before a fire. There were two things in

2

that room I did not like. One was a cat. I hate cats!
I had never seen one before, but I knew I hated it as
soon as I smelled it. It had feet and a tail and gray
fur and yellow eyes, and it lay on a cushion—a velvet
cushion. Elsie held me close beside it.

"See, Gipsey," she said, "this is my new pet—my
dear, beautiful Felix; you must be very good friends.
He is so clever I shall teach him everything. I wanted
to teach you, but you are too lazy and handsome."

Gipsey stretched out her paws, and opened her
mouth in a fearful way. She had claws much sharper
than mine, and strong white teeth. As for promising
to be friends, I did not say anything, but I had my own
opinion about it.

The other thing was a kind of bird. It was large
and green, and had a very wicked look. It was called
Coco, and it laughed and talked. It talked like the
old woman at the crossing who has lost her teeth. It
had a nose like hers, too. It whistled to me, and said,

"Here, you rascal! Oh, get out! get out!"

The grandmother lived in this room. She said,

"You must watch your little dog, Elsie. I cannot
allow him to come in here if he disturbs Gipsey."

DRINKING THE MILK.—Page 19.

"Oh, Felix will not trouble Gipsey," said Elsie, giving me a hug. "They shall be the best of friends."

Gipsey winked at me, and said with her tail,

"Just let me get a chance at you, my dear friend."

And I wrinkled up my nose, and answered,

"I'm ready for you, as soon as my eye-teeth are through."

Neither the grandmother nor Elsie heard anything of this, but Gipsey and I understood each other very well, and so did the bird with the crooked nose, for he laughed, and screamed,

"Ho! ho! you'll catch it, you'll catch it!" Elsie laid me in a cushioned chair and went away. I was very tired, but I was hungry, too, and I was glad enough when she came back with a large basket, and a dish of sweet, new milk. Ah, how delicious it was. I drank and drank without stopping to breathe, and held the dish quite still with my feet, so that I need not spill a drop. Then I took a little run on the soft purple rug, and came back for another drink. Elsie was bringing a cushion for my basket, but the grandmother saw me, and called out,

"See what mischief your dog is doing. He must

not be fed in here; he will ruin everything. Take him to the laundry! It is much the best place for him, and a basket of straw is better than a cushion for the present."

Elsie begged, and even cried, but the grandmother would not hear a word. She said,

" He is only a little beggar, my dear; the laundry will be no hardship to him, and when you have made him a gentleman I shall be happy to see him."

So Elsie carried me away.

IN THE LAUNDRY.—Page 21.

CHAPTER IV.

THE LAUNDRY.

ⓉHE laundry had a stone floor that was very cold, and there was no one to amuse me, but I had a basket of soft straw to lie in, and instead of a basin of bread and milk once a day, my dish was kept always full. I had nothing to do but eat and sleep, and Elsie came very often to see me. Sometimes she took me into the other rooms, and sometimes out-of-doors to play. A very large dog lived in the yard. He had a house all to himself, and he wore a beautiful collar about his neck, with a long chain fastened to it. The other end of the chain was fastened to his house. I suppose that was to keep the house from being stolen. He looked very pleasant, but Elsie never let me go near enough to speak to him. She said he would snap me up like a fly. Once we went on a visit, to see a woman who had been Elsie's nurse. The house was very small, and there were a great many people in it. I have often noticed that small houses have a great many people in them, and large houses only a few. That seems to me very strange, but no one knows the reason, not even the magpie. There was a baby at this house. It did not lie in a cradle, but sat upon the floor. Elsie brought it a cake. I know it was a very nice cake, for I ate it up when nobody was looking. The baby cried, but nobody knew what ailed it. There was a cat there, too, a very small cat, and I chased it out at the door. It jumped in at a little window, without stoping to see that there was a pan of milk in the way. I think some of the milk was spilled, but I did not go in to see.

Afterward I found the baby's shoe under a chair. It was great fun to gnaw it, and I was sorry when Elsie called me away; but she took me to a store, where I met the jolliest little black dog. He was sitting by the door, and he winked at me to let me know he had something to tell me. He lived at a restaurant, and slept outside on the door-mat. Every night when the moon shone the dogs in that street had a party. He invited me to come, and I did not like to tell him that the laundry door was always locked. I thought he was very amusing, but Elsie called him a cur. She said, "Come away, Felix; you must not stop to play with a dirty little cur." The magpie says a cur is a dog who does not have his break-fast brought to him in a dish, but finds it himself, wherever he can. If one could always find plenty to eat it would be very pleasant to be a cur.

When we got home we went into the grand-mother's room, and I lay on the purple rug before the fire, and slept. The cat was not there, but the bird kept saying, "Oh, get out! get out, you rascal!" He was speaking to the grandmother, but she did not take any notice of him.

CHAPTER V.

EXPLORING.

FTER this I was never shut into the laundry, but went wherever I pleased over the whole house—that is, if the doors were left open. The grandmother always shut the doors, but Elsie never did, and there were new places to examine every day. The room I liked best was the one where the people of the house were fed,

BEFORE THE LOOKING-GLASS.—Page 25.

but this room was usually locked. Then there was another with very soft rugs all over the floor, and one day I saw a little dog in there. He looked like the three little dogs at home, and he was running along to meet me, when Judy, the maid, drove me out of the room. I was determined to get in again, and I watched a good many days for a chance, until Judy went in and set the windows open. Sure enough, there was a little dog behind a kind of window. I ran to meet him, and he tried to come to me; but something was in the way, and he could not get out. He was a very saucy fellow, and he mocked me all the time, doing whatever I did. If I could have bitten him I should have been very glad, but Judy only laughed and drove me away.

I have often seen windows like this since then. There was one in the grandmother's room, and another which Elsie lived behind, and Gipsey the cat, and a grandmother. The little dog came there, too, but I never saw the bird. The magpie says these things are our shadows, that creep around after us all day. They live in houses behind these windows, and do exactly what we do; only at night, when we are asleep, they can talk and do as they please. When we dream we only see these shadow-people and what they do, and we think it is ourselves. Often, when I have been very hungry, I have dreamed of a delicious bone, and just as I was about to eat it I would wake and find the shadow-dog had run away with it.

In the next house there were two little children, and they were afraid of me. I could not get through the fence, but I could race up and down upon my own side, and it was such fun to frighten them, almost as good as chasing the hens. Hens make a funny noise when you chase them, but they can fly, and so it soon comes to an end. Elsie scolded me for barking at the children, but I did not hurt them, and I am sure they made a much louder noise. The one with long yellow hair blew on a trumpet, and a trumpet always makes me angry. It makes me howl, though I never knew the reason until yesterday, when the band played in the cemetery. The magpie says it is my nerves, and that all great people have nerves, though he does not know exactly what they are for.

CHAPTER VI.

DREAMS.

I SELDOM saw the cat in those days. Elsie made me a great cushion to sleep on, and it lay in her own room, by a window. It was large and soft, and had tassels at the corners, though I soon pulled them off gnawing at them. She went to a place they called a school, and every day she used to bring me cakes and candy in her pocket. She began to teach me, and I had sometimes to sit up and beg until my back ached, and to practise all sorts of tricks.

She never whipped me, but when I was very good she would give me a bit of cake. She told me I was to perform for her brother when he came home at the holidays, and she expected me to learn to spell by picking out cards with letters on them. I made up my mind I never would do it, but if Elsie had known how performing dogs are trained, she might soon have taught me. They are not trained with cake and candy, but with a whip, and if the children who laugh so much at our funny tricks could see this part of the work, it would not please them so well. I learned a great many other tricks that Elsie knew nothing about. I found out how to open the door, and how to reach things on the table by pulling at the corner of the cloth.

Once I went in the maid's room and took a nap in a nice round box. It had something in the bottom that scratched, but after I shook it very hard, and trampled it down, it did not trouble me. Judy was very angry and whipped me. She said the thing in the box was a bonnet, and that I had spoiled it. I only ate one little piece that tickled my nose. This was the time when I began to have dreams, and for a

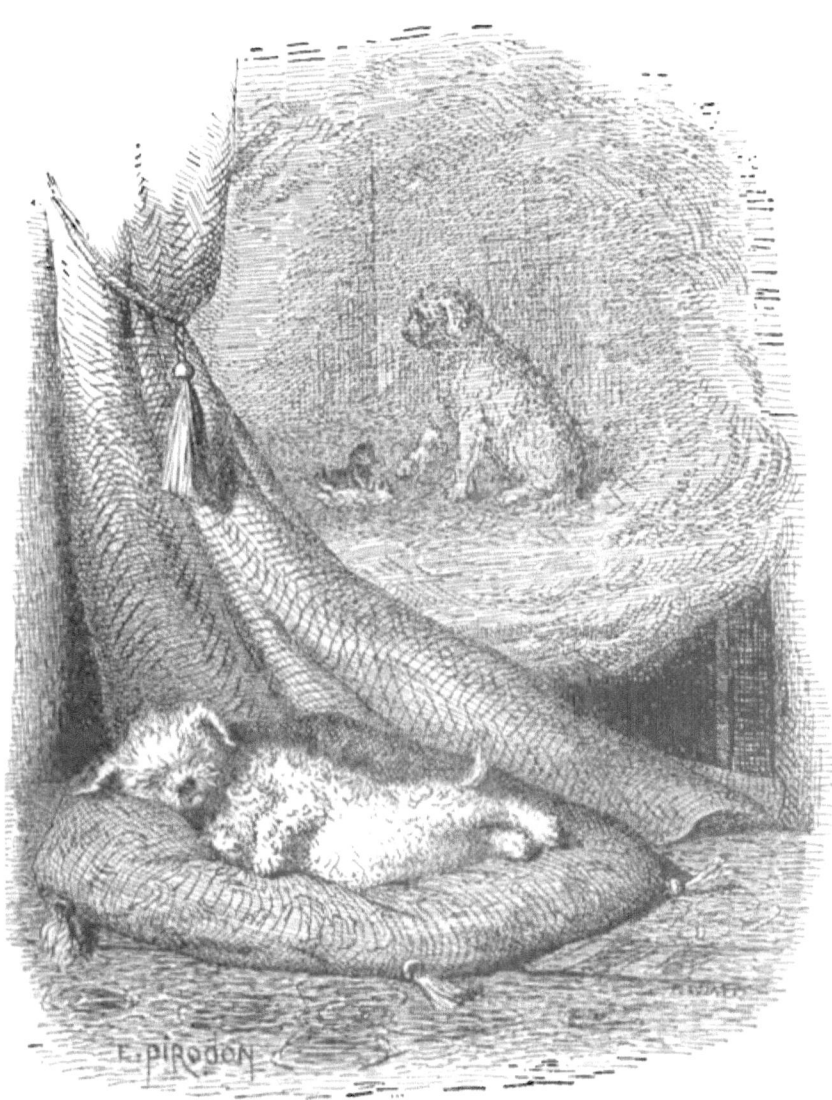

DREAMS.—Page 28.

long time they troubled me very much. When I lay
sleeping on my cushion my mother and the three little dogs often came to see me. I took them all over
the house, even into the grandmother's room, and the
cat was so afraid of my mother's great teeth, that
she did not dare come out from under the sofa. I
took them into the kitchen, and the cook had a plate
of soup and meat ready for us; but just as we took
the first taste, I always waked up, and I was on my
cushion all alone. Then sometimes I dreamed of our
old house, and had such fun racing about in the corners with the three little dogs. There were little
bright streaks of sunshine that came in at the cracks,
and we would try to pick them up in our mouths, but
get nothing. And then we would roll over and over
on the straw, and my mother would tell us stories of
what had happened to her when she was taken about
as a performing dog. Then when I waked again it
made me more sorrowful than ever to find myself all
alone. What made it worse was that I was always
hungry. No matter how much they fed me, I never
had enough, and I hunted all sorts of things to chew.
I ate up one of Elsie's gloves, and half of her reader;

but she never told anybody, and one day I found the
box where she kept the letters she was trying to teach
me, and I chewed them all up and dropped the pieces
through a kind of grate in the corner of the room.

CHAPTER VII.

FUN AND MISCHIEF.

ONE day there was to be a feast. Elsie's papa was coming, and the cook was so busy preparing for the grand dinner she quite forgot to give me any breakfast. Even Elsie forgot me, as she went dancing and singing about the house, but just as I was running out to see if I could pick up a bit in the back yard, Judy pounced upon me and carried me away to the laundry.   There was a great tub full of water, and in spite of all I could do, she dipped me into it, and rubbed and scrubbed me with some dreadful stuff until I was nearly drowned.   I thought Elsie would pity me, but she only laughed, and said,

"Never mind, Felix, now you will have a beautiful white coat, and papa will see how lovely you are."

They shut me up in a warm room until I was dry, and then Elsie put a fine new collar around my neck. I was quite proud of myself, but I tried my best to tell her how hungry I was.   I ate the last tassel off from my cushion, and gnawed a hole in the corner of the sofa, but I did not feel any better.   Then I got the door open and went downstairs.   I found a table spread full of frosted cakes and fresh rolls.   There was a chair all ready for me.   It was too low, but I stood up on the table and helped myself.   There never was anything so delicious, and I tried them all before I could make up my mind which was the best. Some one came in.   It was the grandmother herself, and she was very angry.   She called me a good-for-

HELPING HIMSELF.—Page 32.

nothing, and beat me with her slipper. I had nothing more to eat that morning, but Elsie brought me some of the very same cakes in her pocket.

"Now you have gnawed them, you may as well eat them," she said; "and after all, you did not know any better."

In the evening I was brought down where there were a great many people and bright lights. I saw Elsie's papa. He was a very tall man, and they said he was a soldier. I stood up before him and begged, and he gave me a lump of sugar. He said I was a handsome dog, and advised Elsie to let old Jacques, the gardener, have me to train for her.

"These dogs can be taught to do almost anything," he said. "I have seen a company of them go through all the manœuvres of soldiers on parade."

"But, papa," said Elsie, "I cannot spare my dear Felix, and I know he would not be happy with old Jacques. His house is small, and smells so of tobacco —and then, he might whip Felix; I have heard that dogs are sometimes beaten to make them perform tricks."

"So they are to make them leave off tricks," said

3

the grandmother, "and this little fellow will get many a taste of the whip if he does not mend his manners."

I did not say anything, but I made up my mind then to run away if things were to go on in that fashion. Nothing more happened to me that night, except that I found a lady's fan and tore it to pieces behind the door. It had feathers on the edge, and some of them got in my throat and nearly choked me to death, but Elsie gave me some milk, and that cured me. No one found the fan until the next day, and I heard Judy say it had probably been stepped on. The grandmother looked very hard at me when she saw the pieces, but I pretended to be asleep. I have noticed that grandmothers can tell very well when you have been doing any mischief.

CHAPTER VIII.

WHAT BECAME OF THE DOLL.

EFORE Elsie's papa went away he bought her a doll. It was called a birthday present, although the birthday was already past; and that doll was the beginning of my troubles. It was a very large doll, and when Elsie first showed it to me I thought it was beautiful. It looked almost like Elsie

herself, and it could open and shut its eyes, and I
have often heard it say *mamma* and *papa*. This is
quite true, though the magpie says it is impossible.
The doll was called Lillian, and I soon hated her as
badly as I did the cat. First, because I myself was
Elsie's birthday present, and she had no right to have
another; but most of all, because Elsie loved the
doll the best, and often forgot me for a whole day
together, while she was playing with Lillian, or even
taking her out to walk. The thing I liked best was
to go with Elsie to the park, where were a great
many other children, and where I met some little
dogs that were very good company. We used to go
nearly every day after school, and Elsie was very
proud of me, because no one else had so handsome
a dog. The children always had cakes and candy,
and when I begged for them they would laugh and
shout, and throw me the nicest bits. There were
sparrows in the park—little, tame, brown things, that
hopped about the walks—and a very ugly old woman
sat by the fountain and sold oranges. I did not like
the old woman, and I barked at her. Once I upset
her basket of oranges, and some of them rolled in

the water. Elsie was very sorry, and paid her some
money; but I think she should have taken her basket
away when I was running a race with my friend Don.
Walks are to run on, and not for old women with
orange baskets.

After the doll came, this was all at an end. I had
to wait for my breakfast until Lillian was dressed, and
often my supper was forgotten altogether, while the
doll was shown off and made to roll her eyes and nod
her head.

It was the doll who must go to the park, and
I had to watch my chance and slip out when the
door was opened, or I was left behind. The doll
liked this very much. She used to roll her eyes at
me, and laugh when she lay on Elsie's lap, and once
when Elsie forgot to give me any supper, she laughed
so much that she fell off from the bed, and made a
little dent in her forehead. I should have torn her to
pieces then if no one had been in the room.

One day there was to be a doll's party. The girl
who made the party was Elsie's cousin, and she had a
great many beautiful dolls, but Elsie was sure there
would not be one at the party so handsome as Lillian.

She told her so while she was trying on all her clothes to see what dress was the prettiest.

Don lived at the cousin's house, and though I did not care for dolls, I wanted nothing better than a frolic with Don, and I put my paws up on Elsie's knee to remind her of it. She slapped me on the nose, and said, "There, now, you stupid thing! you have torn the lace on Lillian's dress! I must be sure and leave you at home to-morrow, for there would be no peace with you and Don together."

You should have heard that horrible doll laugh. She was lying flat on her face, and Elsie was sticking pins into her back; but dolls have no feeling, and they enjoy seeing other people uncomfortable. Just then the grandmother called Elsie, and she laid the doll in a chair and ran to her room. I was too angry to wait another minute. I dragged the doll to the floor and pulled her around by her hair, and then, taking her in my mouth, I raced upstairs to the garret. Nobody saw me. There was a place at the edge of the garret floor, under a window—a very deep place, where things went down but never came up. I put the doll in there. She did not fall very far, but caught by her

WHAT BECAME OF THE DOLL.—Page 38.

clothes and hung there. There were a good many other things in the hole—one of Elsie's slippers, and a ball that I used to play with, and the coachman's gloves, and a round red thing that used to lie on the table in the hall. I went downstairs and played in the yard. I saw Elsie go away in the carriage with her grandmother, so I knew she would not miss the doll for a good while. I went up garret and looked into the hole again. It was still there, and nobody could reach it.

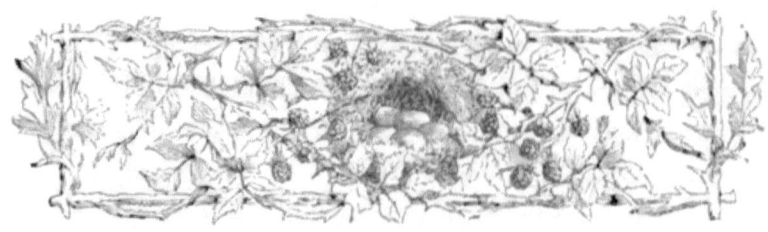

CHAPTER IX.

THE GRANDMOTHER'S SLIPPER.

THERE was a dreadful time about that doll. Elsie hunted everywhere for it, and cried so much that I went up several times to see if I could bring it back. The grandmother said it was stolen, and at last Elsie began to believe it, but she would not have another doll, and she petted and hugged me more than ever. Judy told her a story of a lady whose baby was stolen away by the gypsies. Our cat was called Gipsey, but I do not think she could have stolen a baby. The lady spent nearly all her money in trying to find the baby, and at last it was found by a little dog that used to play with it. After this Elsie wore a black ribbon around her neck, and told all the little girls that the gypsies had stolen her darling Lillian, but she was sure Felix would find her some day. I found her very often. I used to go up to see her when nobody was looking, and I put some more things down there—a pocket-handkerchief of Judy's, and the little box in which the grandmother kept her spectacles.

One day I found the grandmother's slipper—the very one with which she whipped me when I ate the cakes. It was fat and round like the grandmother, and had purple ribbons on it. It curled up its toes, and laughed at me, and the ribbons shook at me. I took the slipper in my mouth and chewed it. I tore the ribbons off, and dragged it away behind a great vase of flowers. Nobody knows what fun it is to little dogs to tear things to pieces, and shake and toss them about. Slippers are better fun than anything else, but the coachman's gloves were very nice. I hid them under the door-mat, and had them buried two days in the garden, before I carried them up garret, I meant to bury the slipper, but the door was shut, and so I hid it behind the pot of flowers. I dug a great deal of dirt out of the pot and covered it up, but the grandmother found it. She said she would put an end to such mischief, and she sent Judy for a stick, and gave me a very hard whipping. The worst of it was, that Gipsey lay upon his cushion and waved his tail, and said, "Now you are getting your deserts, my dear friend. I only hope she will keep on until I tell her to stop."

And Coco laughed and screamed, and swung by one claw.

I did not dare to bite the grandmother, and Coco was always in his cage, but I made up my mind to kill the cat and then run away. I never could understand what cats are good for. They sometimes catch rats, but there are dogs who catch rats for a business, and do it much better, besides earning money for their masters. The magpie says that in some countries the people eat cats, which seems to me a very good way to get rid of them.

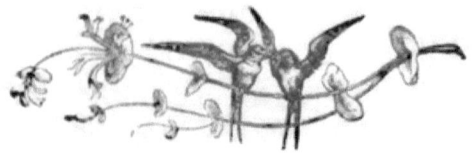

THE GRANDMOTHER'S SLIPPER.—Page 42.

CHAPTER X.

SETTLING A QUARREL.

I DID not wait very long for a chance to settle my quarrel with Gipsey. In a day or two we were left in the room together. I walked around him several times, and he opened his eyes and spit at me. Then I pulled his cushion a little, and he spit again and growled. I dared him to come on, and he came. We had a regular fight. Gipsey had very sharp teeth and

claws, but my hair was so thick and long he did not
have a chance to hurt me much. I chased him all
over the room.   He jumped on the table and knocked
over a tall bottle.   Something sweet was in the bottle.
I tasted it when it ran on the floor.   The coachman
was on the porch.   He looked in the window and
laughed, and seemed to think it was very good fun.
I thought so, too, but Gipsey soon got tired of it, and
tried to find some place to hide.   He jumped on the
table again.   This time it was a bottle of ink that fell
down.   I know it was ink, because it made my feet
black when I stepped in it.   When I chased him down
he jumped into a sort of shelf over the place where
the fire used to be.   There was a little man on the
shelf, standing on one foot.   He had wings like a
goose, but he could not fly, and when he fell down,
one wing and both legs broke off.   I smelt of him and
he was dead.   He was not good to eat.   I tried several pieces while I was waiting for Gipsey to come
down.   Gipsey did not come down at all.   He stayed
up there, and when I got tired watching him I went to
sleep on the rug.

By and by the grandmother came in.   She saw the

SETTLING A QUARREL.—Page 44.

broken bottles and the little man, and she saw Gipsey on the shelf. She went right up to Gipsey and took him in her arms. I thought she would whip him for all the mischief, but she only said,

"Poor old Gipsey! what has happened to you?"

Then she rang the bell for Judy, and they bathed the cat's head with milk, and put something on his ear. His head was very large and round, both eyes were shut up, and a little piece was torn from the top of his ear. They washed the carpet, and threw away the broken things, and then the grandmother said,

"Now I am ready to attend to that dog. I'll warrant he shall do no more mischief in this house."

She fastened a long strap to my collar, and told Judy to tie me up in the coal cellar, and send word to old Jacques that he was either to kill me or give me away within twenty-four hours.

CHAPTER XI.

IN PRISON AND OUT.

UDY was glad of the chance to tie me up, on account of the bonnet, and because I sometimes chased her upstairs and snapped at her heels, when she had both hands full, and could not drive me away. There was only one little window in the cellar, and it was cold and dark. I was very miserable down there, and I wondered what old Jacques would do with me. I wondered if they would give me any dinner before they killed me, and what Elsie would say when she came home and found I was gone. I pulled

IN PRISON.—Page 47.

very hard at the strap, but it only choked me, so I sat still and waited. Every minute I expected to see old Jacques, but the first person who came was Elsie herself. She put her arms around me and hugged me, and called me her dear, lovely Felix, and said I should never be given away. She said we would go away together and find her papa, and live with him. I thought that would be very pleasant, and made up my mind to wait for Elsie to run away with me. She brought me my dinner, and a mat to lie on, and tied her own pretty blue shawl around me before she went back to school. She was so kind I was more sorry than ever about Lillian, but then if we were to run away, it was better not to be troubled with a doll. I waited a long time and Elsie did not come. Then I pulled and gnawed at the shawl, but I could not get it off. I began to chew the strap, and after a little chewing, it came off from my collar. Elsie had left the cellar door open, partly to make it more pleasant for me, and partly because Elsie never did shut doors. I ran up the steps, and went directly out into the back alley. No one saw me, which was very fortunate, but I felt ashamed to be seen with a shawl tied around me as if I were a baby, besides the shawl got under my feet.

At the first corner a kind boy took it off from me. He rolled it up and stuffed it into his jacket, and then he ran away. He seemed to be in a hurry. He went toward our house, and I hope he gave the shawl to Elsie, but I did not stop to see. I ran straight on, through a great many streets, until I was sure old Jacques never could find me. In fact, I could not find myself. I was lost. At first it is not so bad to be lost, especially if you have run away; but by and by you begin to feel that there is no one that belongs to you. You are always looking, and following, and going on, but you never find any one, or get home.

A great dog rushed at me with his mouth open, and I ran between two ladies to get away from him. One of them pushed me away with her foot. Then a boy with a long whip hit me over my ears, and when I sat on a door-step to rest, the maid drove me away with a broom and called me a dirty little cur. I had not noticed before that I was dirty. My paws and my nose were stained with ink, and the sweet stuff in

the bottle had made all the dust stick to my face
and side. I could not find Elsie's school, or the restaurant where the dog lived that invited me to the
party. By and by I came to a corner where an old
man was sitting: he had his eyes shut and held out a
cap for pennies. Some people put pennies in, and
some did not. A little girl put in a cake. I was
standing close by him, and heard the little girl say,

" Is that the little dog that leads you ?"

The man put his arm about me very quickly, and
said,

" Yes ; this is my little dog."

Then he gave me nearly all of the cake, and the
little girl went on.

He took my pretty collar off from my neck and
let me go. The collar was red, and had a gold clasp
and a medal marked with my name. " Felix." I have
seen babies wear such things about their necks ; and
the grandmother had often said it was much too fine
for a dog, and that I should some day be stolen on
account of it.

4

CHAPTER XII.

REFLECTIONS.

THIS chapter is for reflections. The magpie says they always have them in stories, and that they are to make people feel solemn. I think this is a good place to put them in, for nothing in all my life was so bad as the two months that I was lost. It was not so much being hungry—though I was almost starved—as always expecting to be struck or kicked, or to have something thrown at me. To go slinking through the alleys, not knowing what minute a savage dog would pounce upon me ; to be chased and pelted by cruel boys, and to feel from morning till night that I was never for a moment safe, and had no right to be anywhere. When I sat and shivered in the rain, I often remembered my snug, warm home, and wished with all my heart I had not lost it. I almost think the grandmother would have pitied me, and if I had been clean, and could have found my collar, I should have gone back.

I should have liked to begin all over again with Elsie and the grandmother, but dogs never can do that, and they often spoil the world for themselves before they stop to think. The magpie says it is just the same with people, which seems a great pity. I think there should be some way to try it over again.

'Nobody knows how many lost dogs there are in a large city. They live in all sorts of places, and only come out on the streets at night. There was one that lived among some boxes behind a bakery. I stayed with him a good many nights, but he disappeared.

Lost dogs always do disappear after awhile. My mother knew what became of them, but she said I was too young to be told. Besides lost dogs, there are lost children ; at least, I suppose they are lost, for they do not belong to any one. They slip about the streets in the daytime, and at night they sleep under sidewalks, and behind piles of boards, and in cellar-ways, and down on the wharves, and wherever they can get away from the police. They are cold and hungry, too, like the dogs, and nobody feeds them or calls them in. I think it is because in the big houses there are not people enough, and in the little houses there are too many, and so some of them get lost. Sometimes when the children are bigger, they put them in stone houses with iron bars before the windows, and lock them in. Then they cannot get lost again ; but it is not pleasant in houses with iron bars before the windows. I know, for I have been in one, but that was a long time afterward.

I do not know as I have mentioned that this was the time when I lost my name. It was on the medal, and the blind man stole it when he stole my collar. Perhaps it was just as well, for Elsie said that Felix

DOG LOST.

A WHITE FRENCH
POODLE DOG, with a
black spot on his back,
about three months old,
and answers to the name
of FELIX.
    A Reward will be paid
to any one who will re-
turn him to

    14 Arlington Ave.

LOST—Page 52.

meant fortunate and happy. One would laugh to
hear a lost dog called Felix!

Another thing I lost. I do not know the name
of it, but it seemed to be inside of me. It made me
love to run and race, and tear and shake things. It
made everything seem full of fun. There were
always little heads nodding and little faces laughing
at me, in the trees and the bushes and the curtains,
and everything that moved and swung. There were
voices that whistled and called me, and I had to rush
after them up and down the yard, but I never found
them. This is what I lost, and the magpie cannot tell
me anything about it. He says birds have nothing
of the kind, and it was not mentioned in the sermon, but he thinks it may have been owing to my
teeth, because when the rector's children behave very
strangely he has heard it said it was their teeth.

I do not know just how long this dreadful kind of
life lasted. It seems a great while, but when you have
no breakfast or supper you cannot tell when days
begin and end. One time is just like another when
nothing pleasant happens, but the next thing I shall
tell is how I found a new home and a new master.

CHAPTER XIII.

LOST AND FOUND.

THE weather was very hot, indeed, and it was hard to find water when you were thirsty. I saw a great many dogs going about with muzzles over their mouths. A muzzle might do very well if you were sure of your dinner, but how would it be if there were no one to feed you? A great many dogs disappeared every day, and one day I saw what became of them. I made up my

mind then to go somewhere else, where there were
no policemen. The dog that lived with me behind the
bakery came from the country, and he said that in the
country there were no policemen. I thought I would
go to the country, and I ran nearly all night to try
to find the way. In the morning, when it was not very
light, I came where a man was sitting on the steps of
a house, eating something. I was very hungry, and
I could not help sniffing at it as I went by. The man
threw me a little bit, and then another, and another.
Nobody had given me a bit in such a long time that
I could hardly believe he meant to feed me. I think
it was cheese, but I have never tasted any such cheese
as that was since then. Before I knew it the man
had me fast in his arms, and slipped a cord around
my neck. "Ah," I thought, "now I am to disappear."

˙ But the man patted and soothed me, and presently
took me into the house. There were three other men
sitting at a table. They all exclaimed when they saw
me, and crowded around me. One examined my
paws, another looked in my mouth, another drew
my ears through his fingers, and the man who had

brought me in declared I was the greatest prize that had ever fallen to them, and would surely make their fortunes. They gave me as much breakfast as I wanted, and then put me into a little room where there was straw on the floor, and a great drum in one corner. There was a monkey in this room. I had seen a monkey before. A man used often to bring one to the gate, and Elsie gave him money. I did not know what they were going to do with me, but I thought I could ask the monkey all about it.

The man took the monkey with him, and they left me there alone a long time. When the monkey came back he told me I was to be trained as a performing dog, and he said he was very sorry for me, and advised me to go home if I got a chance. When I told him I was a lost dog, he said that made a difference, and that performing was not so bad when you were used to it. I showed him that I could already stand up with my paws crossed on my breast and beg, and he said that was very well for a beginning, but I should have to learn a great deal more. That day they washed me very clean, and painted a brown

LEFT ALONE — Page 56.

spot on my side. I had a black spot on my back, which I thought was much prettier, but they painted that white.

There was a woman in the room who washed me. She said I was very handsome, and should have a fine name. She wanted to call me Monsieur Allegrand, because it would look well on the handbills, but the man said he would have no Frenchman about him, but he would name me after his dear old comrade, Captain Fritz.

The monkey said that Captain Fritz had a wooden leg, and could not turn somersets or dance on a tight rope, but that he could play quite wonderfully on the bugle, and nearly always had nuts in his pocket.

The monkey thought it was a very good name to have, and he supposed Captain Fritz had done with it, for he saw him carried away in a box a long time before, and he had never come back.

One thing I didn't like, and that was the spot on my side. I tried to lick it off, but it was of no use. I had my first lesson that day. My master sat upon a stool, and called me to him. When I came he would

give me a bit of meat, and then send me away again.
I learned two words very well.   They were, "*Come!*"
and "*Go!*"   When I told the monkey, he said I must
be very smart to learn without the whip.

CHAPTER XIV.

TRAINING.

THE monkey was called Major Jack, and sometimes only Jack. We were very good friends and I should have been miserable without him. We had both to go through the same troubles, and we had no time to quarrel. I have noticed that people do not quarrel over their bad times, but over their good ones, and we had no good times to speak of. First there were the exercises every morning. While my master trained us, this was not so bad, but one day another man came in and looked on.   He was very angry about something, and said we did not get on at all, and he would train us himself.

"The first thing to do," he said, "is to make them thoroughly afraid of you."   He took the whip and beat me with it until I thought he would kill me.   I could not get away from him, and at last I only lay on the floor and trembled.   The monkey was beaten also, and he did it not only that day but many days, so that when we heard his dreadful voice we watched without hearing anything else, to see what he was going to do.

After that, the monkey never left his exercise to run after flies, as he sometimes used to do, and you might have offered me the finest bit of meat in the market and I should never have turned my head to look at it while my master's hand said "Attention!"

After we had exercised a long time, if we had done well, we had our breakfast, but if we had not pleased our master we had nothing.   Very often when we were almost starved, the woman gave us something.   She was very kind, and used often to pat my head, and say,

"Poor Fritz! there is only one way out of trouble for you and me, and that is the way the Captain went."

I never knew what she meant, but I knew she would take me with her if she went anywhere, and I made up my mind to stay just as long as she did.

Once she took me with her to market. It was very early, and as we went along the streets only a few people were awake. The people at the market were just unloading their wagons and arranging the things in the stalls. Some of them looked cross and sleepy, and no one paid much attention to the woman.

When the grandmother went to market, every one was anxious to sell to her, but perhaps that was because the grandmother had a new, large basket and a man to carry it, and the woman had a very small basket which she carried herself. I have noticed that it is just the same with baskets as with houses. Those who buy for a good many people often have very small baskets, especially if the people are children, while others buy great baskets full for only two or three.

The woman only bought a small bit of meat and some onions. She looked at other things, and once she asked the price of a basket of fruit, but she shook her head when they told her. Something about the man at the fruit-stall smelled very queer. It made me remember my mother, and our house, and the three little dogs.

The man said,

"You have a fine dog there. Is he trained?"

And the woman said,

"Oh, yes. He was trained in Paris. He is pure blood."

The man laughed a little, and went on arranging his melons; but he said,

"One can tell pure blood. The brown mark on his side shows he is a mongrel."

All at once I remembered this was the man who sold me to Elsie, and who had my mother at home, but the woman hurried me away; and, after all, I could not leave her.

She went home very quickly, and after that I was never allowed to go to market. Sometimes I thought of running away; but by and by I almost forgot that

SLEEPING WITH JACK.—Page 63.

there were other dogs or other places. I only thought of trying to do what my master wanted me to do, so that I might have my breakfast, and then sleep on the straw with Jack.

CHAPTER XV.

THE DANCING-SCHOOL.

AFTER you have learned to stand up for a long time and beg, it is quite easy to learn to dance. I think a dog looks much better walking on four feet than on two; but the people for whom we performed did not seem to think so, and my master took great pains to teach me.

The monkey had a part in all the tricks, and he had much the worst of it; for besides performing, he had to wear a suit of clothes exactly like a soldier.

PERFORMING.—Page 65.

He said the cap made his head ache, and the coat would hardly allow him to breathe, and he had fearful cramps in his legs at night, which I think was on account of the pants. I was always afraid they would make me wear clothes, but they never did. The monkey sat upon a bench when I danced, and played upon a trumpet; and sometimes he waved his trumpet and called out, "Right, left, forward, back." It was not really the monkey who said this, but my master; but every one supposed it was the monkey. I was almost sure of it myself at first. It was my master who made the music, also, with something which he held in his mouth, under his great moustache; but the people did not understand this, and were never tired of laughing and shouting to hear a monkey talk and give lessons in dancing. We had our practice at home, but every afternoon we went about to shops and places where men were eating and drinking, and we were made to perform. Sometimes they gave my master a great deal of money, and sometimes very little. If they gave him much we all stayed at home and rested.

In the evening we went to a larger room, and the

5

other three men went also. There were pictures all
over the front of the house, and my master sat by the
door beating on the drum, and one of the men blew
on a bugle. When I hear a bugle I always howl. The
noise winds round and round in my head. I was
whipped a great many times for howling, but it made
no difference. Something inside of me did it. Jack
sat on his master's shoulders· with his red cap and
coat on. He had his trumpet and pretended to play.
The people all stopped as they came along, and a
great many of them came in. All who came in paid
some money to the man at the door, and when the
room was full, the performance began. There was a
high platform with sawdust all over it. The sawdust
often got in my nose, and made me sneeze. There
were ropes high up in the air, and poles and ladders.
The men took off their clothes and put on some that
were very fine. Their faces were painted, and the
ugliest one, who used to beat me, was so handsome,
when he ran out upon the platform and smiled and
bowed, that all the people clapped their hands at him.
He used to walk on the ropes, and run up the ladders,
and hold the other men on his shoulders, and swing

himself from a ring like Coco the parrot. He smiled
all the time, and when there were ladies in the house,
they often threw bunches of flowers at him. I thought
it was because they wanted him to go away, but the
magpie says it was because they were pleased with
him.

They should have seen him with his old coat on,
lying on the floor in our house, or even in the gutter
when he had been drinking something in a bottle. He
often threw things at the woman, when he came home
—not flowers, but his boots and bottles, and once a
heavy stool. He sold the flowers at a shop. They
gave him more bottles for them.

After the men had gone through a great many
tricks they brought me upon the platform. They
taught me to come in with the monkey riding on my
back.

First I carried him to his stool and waited
until he sat down. Then I stood up and made a bow
to the people, and the monkey took off his cap and
did the same. The people always laughed then, and
clapped their hands, and after they were still, we began to perform.

It seems to me very foolish to laugh so much at a dog and a monkey for doing things which you could do quite easily yourself, but which cost us so much pain and trouble to learn; but the harder work it was, the more they seemed to like it.

CHAPTER XVI.

A MUSICAL EAR.

NE thing which made me a great deal of trouble was my howlings at the bugle. One night when they had taught me a new trick the man played a dreadful tune with his bugle. I knew I should be whipped if I howled, but something began to buzz in my ears and to creep up and down my throat, and by and by I had to open my mouth and let it come out. It was a very loud howl, and the people made a kind of hissing noise like geese. They made that noise when anything did not please them.

That night the man played the bugle until he was

tired out, and whenever I howled, my master whipped
me, but it did no good. They said I had not a
musical ear. I felt very much discouraged, and the
monkey examined my ears carefully, but he said nothing was the matter with them, only he thought they
were too long, and he advised me to let the woman
cut them small and round like his. That only shows
that monkeys are not wise.

The magpie says a great many people have no
musical ear, but they do not howl when they hear a
bugle, so he thinks there must be some way to learn.
I wish I could have found it out, though it does not
matter now. Nobody here is disturbed when I howl,
and the magpie thinks it sounds beautifully.

While we were performing at this place I found a
new friend. His name was Carl, and he belonged to
the man who took care of the house. The man was
old and had white hair, but Carl was small, and loved
to run and climb and jump. He could go up a lad-
der as fast as my master, and hang by his feet to the
bar and turn over and over. The man who beat me
tried to buy him. He said he would give money for
him and train him to perform. Carl said,

"THE MONKEY EXAMINED MY EARS."—Page 70.

"Oh, yes, Grandfather, I should so like to have beautiful clothes and make everybody wonder at my tricks; and I should like to go about with the pretty dog and the funny little monkey, and see so many strange places."

But the grandfather shook his head and kept on sweeping. I think he knew there were other things about such a life that the people who only see the performances know nothing of.

But Carl was a great comfort to me. We played together when they were fixing the ropes and things, and afterward, when I was very tired, he would take my head on his lap and stroke my ears and talk to me. He had a dog of his own, but it was very stupid.

He had a little sister, too, and one day he brought her to see me. She had only poor clothes on like Carl, but she could sing quite wonderfully. She sang a song about a dog, and then Carl made me perform my tricks for her. She was very much pleased, but she was afraid of the monkey.

The man said he should like her, too, and he told Carl if his grandfather ever died he had better take his little sister and come to live with them, so that she might wear beautiful dresses, all over spangles!

Carl laughed, and said he would come; but he never did. I know the reason, and I shall tell it when we come to the right place.

CHAPTER XVII.

NEW TRICKS.

T was very discouraging after I had learned to do one trick quite well, that the people so soon grew tired of it and wanted something new.

I was a long time learning to stand upright, with the monkey on my head, and move slowly about to the sound of the trumpet. This was very hard to do, because the monkey always would forget, and stick his nails in my head to keep from falling.

When we practised I had a stiff iron collar about my neck, with sharp things inside to keep me from moving my head. It made my neck sore, but that only made me more careful to hold my head very still.

The first time we tried this on the platform, every one was amused. There were a great many boys in the house. Some of them were lost boys, and some of them were boys who sold papers and picked up rags and bones in the streets. They always made a great deal of noise, and sometimes they threw things at us.

Once a boy threw an apple and knocked the monkey's cap off. The monkey put it on again with the feather behind, and that only made them laugh the more.

The boy who made the most noise was one that picked up bones. I don't know what he wanted of them, for most of them had been gnawed by lost dogs, besides being thrown out. The magpie does not know either; but there were boys who gathered

NEW TRICKS.—Page 74.

great bags full, and sold them to an old woman who had a very dark shop on an alley. She bought, also, old bottles with nothing in them.

This boy wanted me to dance faster, and he called out to the monkey to hurry up the music; but if you ever tried it, you would know it is not so easy to dance on your hind legs and carry your head straight. Then they all began to stamp and whistle and throw nuts at us; and at last it was so bad I came down upon my feet, and the monkey jumped off and began to pick up nuts. My master came forward and bowed to them, and tried to say something, but they only stamped the louder and threw nuts at him, also. When he found no one would listen, he went away and took us with him.

He sat in the door with his hands over his face. He seemed to be hurt somewhere, but it could not have been the nuts. I was very sorry for him, but when I licked his hands he only cuffed me.

When the other men came home they were very bad. They talked loud, and shook fists at my master, though I do not know what it was about. He was much better than they, and if I could have gone away somewhere with my master and the woman I should have liked it very well.

Afterward we tried the same trick again, and nobody threw anything. But they liked it best when I sat in a chair, with a great ruffled cap on, and held the monkey in my arms. The monkey had on a little cap, like a baby, and a long, white dress. There was a bottle on the table, and a cup; and I held a spoon to his mouth as if I were feeding him. The monkey knocked the spoon away, though there was nothing in it, and my master, who stood out of sight, made a crying noise. All the people thought it was the monkey who cried, and then I put him in the cradle and rocked him. When he tried to get up I boxed his ears, and then his cap came off.

Things often happen in this way when you are performing, and you never know what to do. I took the cap in my mouth and carried it behind the curtain to my master. This was wrong, and the people laughed and stamped to see the nurse running across the platform on four feet, with the baby's cap in her mouth. My master sent me back, and then I found the monkey sitting on the back of the chair, drinking the stuff in the bottle. I took him in my mouth by his long clothes and carried him out. It was quite hard to do, for the long clothes got under my feet; but I think it was the right thing, for even my master laughed very much.

CHAPTER XVIII.

LITTLE MINNA.

ANOTHER thing which I learned to do was to stand upon a little barrel, and make it roll all over the stage by stepping very slowly backward all the time. The monkey rode upon my back and drove me, but he did not like it at all.

WALKING ON A BARREL.—Page 78.

Carl often tried this trick with the barrel, and he could do it quite well. He went much faster than I did, and could even dance while the barrel was rolling, but then he had only two feet to keep in place while I had four, which makes a difference. Carl's little sister was sick. He told me about her, and my master said he was sorry. He went to see her one day and took me with him. He carried an orange in his pocket, and a large picture, like the one on the door of the house where we used to perform, but he left the monkey at home, because Minna did not like the monkey. We went up a great many stairs to the room. When you looked out at the window, you could see the top of another house and a chimney close by. There was a cat sitting by the chimney, but I did not want to chase her. I had left off caring about cats. The grandfather was in the room, and Minna. The grandfather had a hammer and he was driving little sticks into a shoe. He did it very fast, and it made a noise — not a loud noise, but a long noise that never stopped. I was tired of hearing it, and I think Minna was tired, but it went on all the same.

Minna was pleased with the picture, and my master fastened it on the wall where she could look at it. She was pleased with the orange, too, and even the grandfather stopped his hammer a minute to say,

"That is good for my little Minna; she cried for an orange, but folks like us must not choose whether they will live or die. Dying is cheap, but it costs money to live."

Then he hammered faster than ever, and my master put me on the bed by the side of Minna. She laid her hand on my head. It was a very little hand, and it was hot like fire. I remembered that once when Elsie was sick her hand felt like that, but Elsie lay by a window, and had Judy to fan her. She had oranges, too, and grapes, and water with ice in it. I do not like water with ice in it; but Elsie did.

Minna was not so large as Elsie; she was so very little, I think I could have carried her almost as easily as I did the monkey. Afterward we went to see her again, and she was still smaller, and after awhile she was gone. I looked all over the room for her, and then I asked the grandfather where she was. He was hammering just the same, but he stopped a minute and looked at me, and said,

"You miss her, don't you, Fritz? Well, it's a better place where she has gone, and I hope my little Minna isn't lonesome as we are."

Carl looked very sorry. He put his arm about me, but he did not care about playing. I wondered why Carl and the grandfather did not go, too, if it was a better place where Minna had gone, but perhaps they would not let them in. Often, when I was lost, I have followed some one to a door where I could see the light inside, and smell good things to eat, and then the one I followed would step in and shut the door, and it always seemed worse outside after that.

Perhaps when Minna went in, they shut the door and left Carl and the grandfather out. The magpie thinks she died. He says there was something in the sermon about a very good place where people who died sometimes went. It must be that only a few go there, for they bring the most of them here to the cemetery.

6

CHAPTER XIX.

THE BIRTHDAY PARTY.

HE woman at our house sometimes went to other houses to work. Once when the men were away, she took me with her to a very fine house, not at all like ours. It was even more beautiful than the grandmother's house where Elsie lived. There were two little boys at this house, or else they had one boy and two of him, I do not know how it was.

No matter how many people you meet, they have different eyes and mouths. They speak differently and they smell differently; but these boys were alike in everything. I thought at first that one was a shadow-boy, but he was not. I heard the cook say they were twins, and one was called Alfred, and the other Arthur. They came to the laundry to see me, and wanted to take me all over the house, but the woman kept me with her. She told the cook that she was afraid of losing me, and if she lost me, my master would beat her. She said I had once run away and made a good deal of trouble, and it would take the bread out of their mouths if such a thing were to happen again. It was true that I ran away, but I do not see who told the woman about it.

The cook said she supposed dogs were a great deal of trouble, and so were children. They must always have something new going on. There were seven at that house, and some one was always having a birthday party.

It was lucky that the boys were twins, and could have but one birthday between them, so it saved just half the bother. The rest were all over, but the twins were to have a birthday party the next week, and there would be fine doings.

By and by a bell rang and a girl came to say her
mistress wished to see the woman and the little dog.
The woman wiped her hands, and we went upstairs.
The mistress was in the room where the little boys
lived, and there were balls and hoops, and little
wooden houses, and a horse that rocked, and a
dog with wheels on his feet. Both the boys ran to
me, and patted me, and when the woman told me to
dance for them I did it. The lady was very kind.
She laughed at me and gave me a cake from a basket
on the table. There were more cakes in the basket
and she gave them all to the woman and told her they
were for her children at home. The woman thanked
her, and said there was only little Jack, but he was
very fond of cakes.

Then the lady asked her all about me, and what
tricks I could perform, and said she wanted my master to bring me to the house the next week when the
twins had their birthday party, so that the children
might see me. She said there must be no doubt
about it, and that she would pay a great deal of
money. When the woman heard of the money, she
said he would come, and bring both me and Jack.

"Very well," said the lady, "I suppose he needs Jack to help him. Has he any suitable clothes?"

When she knew that Jack was the monkey, she laughed very much, and said she thought he was a boy.

My master was very much pleased to hear of the birthday. He made us practise a great deal, and taught us a new trick with hoops. My part was quite easy, but it was hard for the monkey to hold the hoops still, and when he moved them the least bit it spoiled everything.

It was dark when we went to the birthday. My master carried me in his arms, because I had been washed very clean, and had my spots painted over. We waited in a little room by ourselves, but sometimes when the door was open I could see the great room was full of children, walking about and playing. By and by we went out where there was a stage covered with carpet, and curtains hung before it. When we were ready, they drew the curtain, and then I saw two long rooms full of children, and some ladies, but only one gentleman. He was the man that the twins belonged to, and he had one on each knee. They jumped up and down when they saw us, but when we began to dance they all sat still. We did every one of our tricks for them, and the monkey held the hoops beautifully ; but what pleased them most was when the monkey was dressed for a baby, and I was the nurse. I think myself that is very good, only the cap always made my ears itch.

After it was all over the children came to see us, and Jack and I ran about the room. We had a very good time, but a boy stepped on my foot, and we ate so much cake that we were both quite sick in the night.

The magpie says people who go to parties always do that, and you have to get used to it. If I had been a boy I suppose I should have got used to it, but dogs are different.

JUMPING THROUGH HOOPS.—Page 86.

CHAPTER XX.

TRAVELLERS.

WHILE we were at the party something happened—I do not know what; but when we got home the other men were gone, and the woman was alone in the dark. I heard her say something about the police, and I suppose they had taken them away. I have seen them take people away, and I think they drown them; at any rate, that is what they do with the lost dogs when they catch them, though the magpie says people cannot be got rid of like dogs when they are troublesome. I do not see why, for I have never seen dogs do so much mischief as men sometimes do.

Very early the next morning the man called us out of our room and gave us our breakfast. He was eating his breakfast, too, and the woman had a shawl and a little bundle. She sat down by me and talked to me. I knew something was going to happen, because she was usually too busy to talk to me.

I licked her hand, and she said, "I should like to take you with me if I might, Fritz. I believe you are the only one who cares at all for me."

Afterward my master took his drum and blanket, and called Jack, and we went away. The woman went out, too, and shut the door, but she did not go with us.

We went on all that day; only once we stopped in the street, and my master went into a house and brought out some bread and meat. It was cold and rainy, and we shivered very much while we waited for him.

That night we all slept together in a barn. There

MDE VINS

SPIRIDON

STOPPING IN THE STREET.—Page 88.

was plenty of hay, and it was very warm and comfortable, but the monkey cried. His head ached, and he
was very sick. It was partially the nuts and candies,
and partly the cold from being out in the rain.

In the morning we went on, and the monkey rode
on the drum and had the blanket over him.

We came to another town in the evening, and my
master carried the monkey to a house where were a
great many bottles. There were some men, and they
all laughed at the monkey. But one man, with white
hair on his face, took him in his arms and looked at
him very kindly. I watched to see that they did not
hurt Jack. They fixed something in a cup and made
him drink it. Then the man asked my master some
questions, and afterward we went away.

We slept in another barn that night, and in the
morning the monkey would not wake up; he was
dead. My master was very sorry, and he lay down
on the hay a long time. I could not see his face, but
I licked his hand, and I tried to wake Jack up.

After awhile my master carried Jack out. He
put him under his coat, and we went a long way, to a
place where there were no houses and a great many

trees.   He made a place in the ground and put Jack in and covered him up.   I did not like that, and I was sure Jack would not like it, and I whined and cried, and scratched the dirt away.   But my master went on, and I had to follow.

We went back to the same town where they gave Jack the medicine, and I tried some of my tricks on the street corners, but I could not do much without Jack, and we got very little money.

My master sold Jack's coat and cap, and the stool and trumpet to a man who went about with a box on his shoulders.   The box had a handle, and when you turned the handle it made a dreadful noise—much worse than the bugle.   It was so dreadful that people opened their windows and gave the man money to go away.   I should think the best way was to call the police and have the man drowned.

CHAPTER XXI.

THE WHEEL OF FORTUNE.

THINGS began to go very badly with us about this time. We had no house, but were always wandering about. I was often nearly as hungry as when I was lost, and sometimes my master lay and slept all day.

He sold the drum, also, and the blanket, so that we were often cold at night; and at the places where we went they gave him a great deal to drink, but very little to eat, and no money.

At last we stopped at a very large house a little way out from town. It was called a tavern, and the men who went into town with wagons, to sell fruit and vegetables and grain at the market, often stopped there to feed their horses and to eat.

My master took care of the horses in the barn. It was a very good place to live, and we had plenty to eat; but there was a big boy who teased me a great deal.

This boy had to work in a room called a dairy, where they made butter and cheese. I sometimes ran in there to lap up the milk that was spilled on the floor, and I saw the boy at work turning a kind of handle. That was the way they made butter, and they called it churning. There were two women in the room who helped to make the butter.

The boy said I could be taught to churn, and that he meant to teach me. After that I was careful not to go into the dairy, but he made a kind of wheel with

IN THE WHEEL.—Page 93.

steps inside and fastened it up in the barn. He put
me in this wheel and when he began to turn it, I had
to step forward a little, and then to keep on stepping,
and after awhile I saw that the wheel turned of itself
when the boy did not touch it. I never felt anything
so uncomfortable; always to be scrambling up and
never get to the top. It was the worst of all tricks,
because you could not stop, and because it never was
finished. The boy was very much pleased. He
rolled on the floor and laughed, and called all the
men to see.

"Now," said he, "I will get my father to attach
the wheel to the big churn, and then Captain Fritz
shall do the work while I do the play."

After that, I kept out of his way as much as I
could, but whenever he caught me he would put me
in the wheel. I never had to churn, because the
father would not allow the wheel to be put in the
dairy. He only shook his head, and said, "Tut, tut!
The less time for work the more time for mischief. I
shall not spend money on machines so that a stout
boy may be idle. Boys were made for work; dogs
were not."

I was curled up in the manger when he said this, right under the nose of Jerry, the gray horse. Jerry and I were good friends, and when we heard what the father said he winked at me, and we laughed quite heartily.

I think we stayed at the place several years, until my master left off doing his work well, and the father and the men with the wagons used often to scold him very hard. Sometimes he went away and was gone all day, and Jerry told me that often he had not a drop of water from morning until night, and that once Brown Bess had no oats for a week, and he heard them say my master had sold them for drink. I could not understand this, for there was a pump in the yard with a large trough always running over with cool water, but Jerry said that what he drank was something in a bottle. I suppose that is what the man who beat me used to drink. It makes people cross and sleepy.

I heard them say that my master would be sent away, which made me very sorry; but I hoped it would not happen.

CHAPTER XXII.

OFF AGAIN.

OMETHING much worse happened, for one night a rough man, with a very surly voice, came to the tavern and asked leave to stay all night. The moment I heard his voice I knew it was the man who used to beat me, and I ran out to the barn and hid in Jerry's manger.

By and by my master came out, and then I heard

some one talking with him. It was that man. They
sat upon the hay and talked very low, but I heard
them say they would take me and go a long way off,
and I should perform for them again. I do not think
my master wanted to go, but he was afraid of the
man. The man said he had bought another monkey,
and he showed him some pictures he had made to
hang on the outside of the house. I looked at them,
and so did Jerry. There was one in which I was
nursing the monkey, one where I was rocking him in
the cradle, and one where I was playing on a flute.

I did not care about the others, but I knew I never
could learn to play on the flute, not if he killed me.
After the man went away, I talked with Jerry about it.
Jerry knew a great deal about performing.

Brown Bess, his mate, was once in a circus, and
she had told him, and he said it was a very bad life
for any one. . It spoiled the people, and it spoiled the
horses. Bess would always have a stiff shoulder on
account of what she had gone through. The worst
of all was the children. I could hardly believe the
dreadful things that Bess said about the children that
are taught to perform, and I was more glad than ever

PLAYING ON A FLUTE.—Page 96.

that the grandfather did not let them have Carl and little Minna.

Jerry advised me to go away somewhere, until my master had forgotten about the pictures, and then come back. He said the market-wagons began to go by long before daylight, and I could follow them to the town. I made up my mind to do it, and I thought it quite likely I might find the grandfather and Carl. I knew they would be glad to see me, and perhaps would let me live with them. I followed the very first wagon in the morning. There were two horses, and it was quite hard to go so fast, but I ran a little way behind until it was daylight, and then I kept under the wagon. No one seemed to notice me, and I followed until they came to the market.

It was just as Jerry had said; this was the very town where I used to live, and after I came to the market I knew the way to a great many places.

If you do not wish to appear lost, it is necessary to go right on, neither too fast nor too slow, but as if you had business. I went to our old house, but no one lived there, and there were workmen beginning to pull it down. I could see the little room where Jack

7

and I used to sleep. There was a pile of stones and rubbish in it.

Then I tried to find our performing-house, but all that street was taken away, and in its place was a wide street, with rows of tall, fine houses. I began to fell very sad, but at last I came to the street where the grandfather lived. That was not taken away; the gutters, and the broken sidewalks, and the high stairs were just the same.

I went up the stairs and waited at the door a long time. I thought Carl would be coming home soon, or the grandfather would come out to look for him. But no one came, and I could not hear any hammering.

At last an old woman with a cane came up the stairs and unlocked the door. I followed her into the room, but the grandfather was not there; it was quite empty. The woman sat down on a stool and looked at me. She looked very sad, but she spoke kindly. She said, "I believe you are lost, but you must go somewhere else for a home. I have not so much as a crust to give you." She opened the door again and I went out. I waited and waited, but the grandfather did not come, and so I went away.

CHAPTER XXIII.

A STREET BEGGAR.

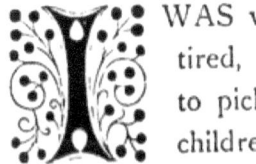 WAS very tired, and more hungry than
tired, but there seemed to be nothing
to pick up. Where there are so many
children the dogs have a poor chance.
I found a bone, but it was quite dry, and at last I

came to a shop with large windows filled with delicious
things. There were fresh rolls of bread, and cake,
and pies, and inside, upon long tables, were such things
as my master sometimes bought when he had plenty
of money. The man who sold the things sat in the
door. He had on a white apron, and he was smoking
a pipe. I remembered how I had earned many a
dinner at such places for my master, and I thought I
might as well try for myself. So I stood up before
the window and looked straight at the bread and
begged, and then I ran up to the man and begged
again. He laughed at me, and called his wife to see.

She said I was a very amusing beggar, and should
have my pay; so she brought me a large plate of
bones and scraps, from a room where men were eating. I was much obliged to her, but I did not like the
sound of the men's voices, and as soon as I had eaten
I ran away. I went to our old home. The workmen
were gone, and I crept into a corner and slept there.
Afterward I stayed about there a good deal, and
sometimes the workmen gave me bits from their dinner. I heard them say that I probably belonged to
some of the families that had been turned out of the

BEGGING FOR BREAD.—Page 100.

old building, and that it was very wonderful how dogs
would remember their homes and come back to them.
Once, when they were eating, a workman's cap blew
off from his head, and the wind carried it a long way
down the street, but I caught it and brought it back to
him, and made him a bow. This pleased him very
much, and he told the men of tricks he had seen done
by dogs, when he was a boy, in England. I could have
done them, every one, but I lay still and looked very
stupid, for I never meant any one to know that I had
been a performing dog.

"Yes," said another man, "but that is nothing at all
to what I have seen done by a performing dog in this
country. She was called Lady, and she was the most
celebrated dog in the world. She was taken everywhere, even to Paris, and every one went to see her;
but she was hurt in some way that ruined her. I
think she died several years ago."

That was the way I first heard that my mother was
dead. I had always hoped that some day I might go
and see her again, but it was fortunate that I became
acquainted with her as soon as I did, or we should
never have met at all.

That day the workmen finished tearing down the walls, and at night I had no place to sleep, and then I began to be lonesome, and to wish for my master. I followed one of the men to his home, and when he went in I sat on the step. After awhile a little girl saw me. She was eating something, and she called me under the window and threw me a bit. Then the man came with a baby in his arms, and whistled to me. The baby laughed and clapped its hands, but presently they all went away, and nobody asked me to come in. That night I came near getting into trouble. I was hunting for a bone in an alley and two boys caught me. One said,

" This dog is lost, and there will be a reward offered for him. Let us keep him and get the reward."

But the other said, " There will be no reward; you can see his hair is dirty and matted; he must have slept in the streets a long time. Let us take him to old Tom—he will give us a quarter for him."

They shut me up in a little coal house, and they sat on a bench outside, and talked about what they would do with the money. One said,

" A quarter is not much; old Tom gets a great

deal more for the skins when he has tanned them. If
we only knew how to tan the skin ourselves."

So I found out that old Tom wanted my skin to
tan. I do not know what tanning is, but I was sure
I could not get on at all without my skin; so, as soon
as the boys went away, I opened the door and ran as
fast as I could. Jack taught me to open doors, and it
is very easy if they are the right kind of doors, but
sometimes they are not. The right kind of door has
a thing to go up, and you only have to push it a little,
and the door opens.

CHAPTER XXIV.

IN A CAGE.

THE next day I hurt my foot, and for a long time I was lame, and could not run fast enough to get out of the way when things were thrown at me. This was the time when I saw the grandmother and Elsie. I was sitting on the curb-stone, and thinking that as soon as my foot was well I would go back to my master, when an elegant carriage stopped close by me. It was the grandmother's carriage. I knew the coachman, though he had some new gloves, and the grandmother, though she had windows over her eyes. Then some one got out of the carriage and went into a shop. I was sure it was Elsie, though she was very tall and straight—quite as tall as Judy the maid used to be. I followed her into the shop, and kept close to her, and a man said, "Is this your dog, Miss?"

And Elsie turned and looked at me, and drew back her dress, and said, "That dirty creature! no, indeed!" and then the man kicked me out at the door.

My back was hurt, and my foot lame, and something inside of me ached just as it did when Elsie took the doll to walk and left me at home. I could not bear it that Elsie had forgotten all about me. I sat down and looked at the carriage, and by and by the grandmother said,

"John, do you remember a little dog that Elsie had when she was a child—a puppy that ran away, or died?"

"'Pears like I recollect something about it," said John.

"Well," said the grandmother, "I think that dog out there is something such a dog."

"I can't say, ma'am, what he might a growed into," said John, snapping his whip at me; "that dog is an uncommon low-looking animal to my eye."

I knew John pretended not to remember me for fear the grandmother would take me home; and when I saw Elsie coming out, I determined to try once more. So I limped up to her, and put my paws up on her dress; but she only screamed, and said,

"Drive him away, John; he must be mad! I can't abide dogs."

"You used to like them well enough," said the grandmother. "Have you forgotten the puppy you almost broke your heart over?

"That was long ago, before I knew there were better things to break one's heart over," said Elsie. "Let me see, what was his name?"

"Seems to me it was Frisk," said the grandmother.

"Oh, I remember, it was Felix," said Elsie, and just then the shopman brought out the bundles, and they drove away.

After that I did not care what became of me. I

IN THE CAGE.—Page 107.

had lost my master and Jack, and Carl and his grandfather, and even Elsie. I should have liked to creep into Jerry's manger and die; but as I was limping down the street, all of a sudden something whizzed over my head, and jerked me across the side-walk.

There was a policeman on the corner, and he had thrown a noose over my neck. I expected to be killed at once, but I did not care very much. The policeman took me to a little cage, with iron bars across the front, and put me in. There were a great many of these cages, and nearly all had lost dogs in them.

Some of the dogs were very dirty, and some were clean and handsome, and had fine collars on. Some of them howled and cried, but I only lay still upon the straw, and watched to see what would happen.

CHAPTER XXV.

A NEW MASTER.

OME of the dogs were taken away before night. One was a coach-dog. He was very handsome and would not lie down on the dirty straw; but he was a coward, for he shivered and whined until a man came and claimed him.

Another was an ugly little poodle, that looked like the mop Judy used in washing windows. I thought nobody would want him, but a lady took him away in her arms, and seemed as fond of him as if he had been a baby. Seeing a good many dogs taken away made me wish somebody would come for me, and I watched every one that came, but no one even looked at me. By and by it began to grow dark; I have never seen such darkness as that was; it was outside and inside of me, and seemed to choke me to death. Then a dog in the next cage began to howl, and I howled, too. There was a woman passing by, leading a child. I heard her say, "Poor beasts, they cry like lost children; seems as if they had the sense to know what was coming to them."

In the morning two policemen came into the yard, and an old man followed them. He had a stick, and he walked slowly and carefully, as if he could not see.

The policemen looked into several of the cages and talked together, but the old man did not say anything until he came close to my cage; then he spoke, and I knew it was the grandfather. His hair was very white, and his teeth were gone, and he stooped down as if he was looking for something. When I saw him I

could have torn the cage down, I was so glad. One
of the policemen said,

"Here is the very fellow for you, daddy—a French
poodle; they are easy to teach, and, I declare, he acts
as if he knew some of us."

They opened the door, and I ran to the grandfather
and licked his hands, and jumped about him in spite of
my lame foot, until the policeman said,

"Don't be rough with your greeting, you'll knock
the old fellow off his pins."

The grandfather sat down and passed his poor old
hands all over me, and then he asked if I had a brown
spot on my side.

"No," said the policeman, "but he would have a
black spot on his back if one could see it for the dirt."

The grandfather shook his head. "I thought it
might have been an old acquaintance," he said, "but I
am not so happy as even to have a dog left to remember me."

"Well, daddy, if you are suited, take him away,"
said the policeman, and he put a strap about my neck
and gave the grandfather a cord to lead me by. I
thought now I should surely find Carl; but when we

LEADING THE GRANDFATHER.—Page 111.

came to the little room where he lived, Carl was not
there. There was only a chair and a table and a pile
of straw. On the table was a loaf of bread, and the
grandfather ate some himself and gave some to me.
Now I began to have a home, for I had a master
who loved me. When I was licking his hand, he said,

"Good fellow, we will be comrades now. We are
two that are not wanted in the world, so we will make
our way together. I am glad Carl does not know
about it."

When he talked of Carl I was so wild that he
nodded his head to me, and said,

"Yes, you are Fritz—my boy's old Captain Fritz.
Whatever they say about the spot, I am sure of that.
I can tell an old friend without my eyes."

After that I was contented. We slept together,
we ate together, and I learned to lead him about the
streets and carry a little dish in my mouth for pennies.
Sometimes, when he rested, I would stand up and beg,
with the dish in my mouth, and we got a great deal of
money every day.

Before it was cold weather the grandfather had a
better bed, with blankets to cover him ; but I always

slept at his feet—he would have been cold without me.

There was a girl, too, who used to come in and make the fire, and sometimes she brought a bowl of hot soup for the grandfather.

The grandfather told her about his little Minna, who would have been a stout girl if she had stayed with him, but he was very glad she had gone to a better place. He told her about Carl, too, and then I found out what became of him. His uncle had taken him away to be a soldier, and they had sometimes sent money to the grandfather, but for a long time no letters had come. The grandfather was very sick, and was taken to the hospital, and when he came out his eyes were spoiled, so that at last he was blind.

"But it does not matter," he would say, "now that I have good Fritz to take care of me. They will send for me presently to go to my little Minna, and there they'll make me all over new. Think of that, Fritz—to be made all over new, and better than new. It seems a pity you couldn't have a share in the good times over there. I'm sure you have well earned it, old comrade."

One morning we slept very late. The girl came in and made the fire, and I went and lay down on the hearth. By and by she came back with the hot soup.

"Here is your breakfast, Grandfather," she said.

The grandfather did not wake up, and so she set it on the table, and went nearer to the bed. "Grandfather," she called, "Grandfather!" He did not answer her. He never answered her again. He was dead, and they had sent for him to come to Minna, and he could never go and be made over new again.

8

CHAPTER XXVI.

A NEW SORROW.

NO one seemed to care that the grandfather was dead. Some men came to see him, and they sat upon the table and talked and laughed. A woman came, too— a very old woman, with a cap like the one I used to wear when I nursed the monkey. One of the men told her that her turn would come next, but she did not say anything. He did not know that she was deaf, and I have heard the grandfather say that was worse than to be blind. She looked at the grandfather, and said to herself,

"Aye, he sees well enough now; and there are things worth seeing, too."

I could not tell what she meant, for his eyes were shut, and the room was just the same as ever.

By and by another man came, and he talked to the girl a long time. I think he was angry, for he spoke loud, and thumped on the floor with his cane, but the girl was not afraid of him. She stood up very straight, and looked in his face, and said always the same thing,

"He wanted to be buried at St. Angelo, and he gave me the money to pay for everything. Here is the paper, and it shall be as he said. Some day, he said, Carl would come and plant a flower over his grave."

One of the men who lived in the house said,

"Yes, it shall be as he said. You need not grudge him a decent place to rest in, now he is dead."

So the man went away, and the next day they

put the grandfather in a box and carried him down the stairs. I kept close to them, and when they put the box in a carriage, I thought perhaps they were going to take him to the place where he would be made new again.

I had not begun to be sorry then, because I did not know what would happen, and I thought if I kept close by the grandfather it would be all right. It was a very long way that we went, and after awhile I began to know that I was hungry. When the grandfather would not wake up to take his soup, the girl sat the basin down for me.

" Here," she said, " it is a pity to waste it, and you are his best friend." But I would not eat it. The grandfather always ate first, and left a portion for me, and I could not eat until he did. After that no one thought to feed me.

When we came to St. Angelo I knew it must be the place where the grandfather wanted to go. It was so warm and sunshiny, with green grass and fountains and flowers. I knew the grandfather would like it, and I waited for them to take him out of the box. They did not take him out at all; they set the

WATCHING AT THE CEMETERY.—Page 117.

box by the side of a deep hole, and then, all at once,
I remembered what became of Jack. I jumped on the
box and cried and howled, but they drove me away,
and they buried the grandfather deep down in the
ground. I could not see him ; I had lost him, and it
broke my heart. That was trouble. It was not like
being lost, or being cold or hungry. It was not like
being beaten, or anything else that ever happened to
me. I did not feel anything or know anything but
sorrow, but I lay down with my head close upon the
ground, and waited and listened. I thought he might
move or speak. They would not let me stay by him.
The keeper dragged me away and shut the gate.
That was no worse—nothing could be any worse;
but I· stood up and looked through the gate and
watched the place as long as I could see. When it
was dark I laid down by the gate. I was no more
hungry, and when I shut my eyes I saw great shining
things sailing along in the dark, like lanterns, only
some of them had faces—the face of the man who
beat me, and of my old master, and of the big boy
who made me turn the wheel.

CHAPTER XXVII.

MORE DREAMS.

IT rained that night, and I licked off the drops that fell on my paws. The rain made a little stream that ran along in the gutter close by. It sounded good, but I did not want to go so far to drink. By and by the keeper came along with a lantern. He looked at me, and I think he called me; at least some

DREAMING.—Page 119.

one called, and it sounded away off. Then he brought
a piece of blanket and threw over me. The shining
things came very fast. They were like great bubbles,
and as they sailed by all the faces scowled at me, and
that made me have dreams. I saw my old master,
he was sitting in the door, and I tried to creep past
him, but he caught me. I saw Jack, also, and we lived
in the old house and had our practice together, and
nothing ever went right. When I tried to dance I fell
over, and when I jumped at the hoops I missed them
and went down and down into a place that had no
bottom to it. And always I heard the crack of the
whip, and the voice of the man that beat me, shouting,
"Forward! right! left!" Then I was in the wheel,
and my feet were so tired they would not move, but
clung to the bars, and the wheel turned over and over,
and never for a moment stopped. And then I was in
the cage, and all the dogs howled at me. The policeman said, "*This dog has no master,*" and all the dogs,
and the people that went by, kept saying, "No master! no master! no master!" In the morning the
faces went away and the dreams. Some one opened
the gate, and I tried to crawl through, but I was too

weak to move. A man came and looked at me, and called the keeper. He said to the keeper, "This dog must be taken away; he is half dead."

I was glad when I heard that; I thought if I were dead, too, perhaps I might find the grandfather again.

The keeper said,

"I will not have him killed; I will take him home and Mollie shall nurse him. They brought his master here yesterday, and the poor fellow is dying of grief."

He carried me away to a shed where the rain could not come on me, and then he called Mollie. She is very wise. She is the mother of the house, and takes care of her two little sisters, because the other mother died when they were babies. They wanted her very much; but a great many people die who are wanted very much, and then you have to find out some way to do without them. The way they found out was Mollie. She took care of the little sisters, and she took care of me.

She has a voice that makes you mind; not a loud voice, but one that goes in, and says it over again inside of you. She made me a comfortable bed, and bathed my head and paws with water. She brought me something in a basin, and when I would not eat, she took my head in her lap, and said, " Poor fellow, I know all about it!" and after that I tried to drink a little.

Her voice made all the ugly faces go away, and only pleasant ones come. The two little sisters came and looked at me, but they were afraid, and held their hands behind their backs. The keeper came, too, and he said,

"Do you think you can save him, Mollie?"

And Mollie said,

"I hope so, father; he is more tired and grieved than sick."

CHAPTER XXVIII.

COMFORT.

AFTER that I had pleasanter dreams. I saw the drum and the trumpet, but my master was never there; only Jack and I lay and slept all day in the sunshine, and were very warm and comfortable.

I saw the grandfather, also; he sat in his chair, and I lay at his feet. Carl was there, and Minna. Minna sang the little song about the "Very old dog that went to market," and Carl tied the grandfather's cap upon my head. They all laughed very much, but when I opened my eyes, I only saw Mollie singing to the two little sisters.

I dreamed about the grandmother's house, too. I lay on my purple cushion, and Elsie brought me my breakfast, and put my collar around my neck, and called me her dear, beautiful Felix. I heard her, and

BETTER DREAMS.—Page 122.

I felt the collar; but when I opened my eyes she was not there, and there was something in my throat that choked.

I cannot quite understand about dreams, though the magpie says it is very plain to him, and that it is only the shadow-people having our good times and our bad times over again. I can understand about the good times, but what do they want of the bad ones? How do they know where to find us, and when we die, are they dead, too? The magpie cannot tell this part, and he says it is not necessary to know everything.

He is watching for another sermon, and yesterday he came very near getting one, which blew out at a window, but the rector himself came to get it. He thinks if he could get that it would tell all the things we do not know.

I hope he will find one, for there are a great many things that I do not know. When I had to find my own breakfast and supper, and when I worked for the grandfather, I never used to think about these things; but now I have nothing to do but sit in the door of my house and wonder. I wonder about the people who come here, and about the white doors all over the cemetery, that nobody ever opens, because they do not belong to houses, but little green heaps with grass growing over them. Sometimes, when the moon shines very bright, and I cannot sleep, I walk all about among them, and they are always the same. There is no door where they put the grandfather, but the grass grows there, too, and it is a very sunny corner. I think there should be a door, because some day he might want to come away.

And I wonder about the lights all over my head at night; who lights them, and who puts them out in the morning? The moon goes away to another place, for I have often watched it going and coming, but the little lights that they call stars do not go. They are lighted and put out.

And I wonder a great deal about noises. Who is it that cries so on dark nights when the wind blows? I have heard it everywhere; here in the cemetery, and in the barn where Jerry lived, and even in the grandmother's house. I used to think it was something that was lost, but the magpie says it is the wind itself. Who is the wind, and why does he cry?

CHAPTER XXIX.

THE END.

 AM now coming to the end of my story, because the magpie must help to build his house next week, and then there is not much more to tell.

After awhile things stop happening to you. Mollie was so patient she never grew tired of taking care of me, and even the little sisters learned not to be afraid of me.   They had a doll, and they often brought it to see me, but I never wanted to shake it.   I never want to shake anything now, not even Mollie's cat, who sometimes looks in at the door of my house in a neighborly way.   I think that part of me was lost, too, or else the shadow-people had something to do with it.

The keeper built me a house himself.   He said it looked respectable to have a dog's house near one's cottage.   The house is very comfortable, and it is also pretty; I often hear the visitors speak about it.   It has a tree growing over it that sometimes is all over red with roses.   I do not care for flowers myself, but this pleases Mollie, for she put it there.   She has one like it growing over the window of the cottage, where she sits and sews.   It is a very long time since I came here, and the little sisters do not play with their doll now.   I do not think they know where it is, but I do. They left it on the ground behind my tree a long time ago.   There was just room for it to lie between the tree and the house.   I heard one of them say that the doll was hiding from the Indians, who had burned her house.   That was a day when the leaves were blowing about, instead of staying on the trees, and the doll was covered up under a little heap of leaves.

The Indians never found her, and no one ever came to take her away. By and by the snow came down and covered the leaves up, and now there is only a little brown spot, partly dirt and leaves, and partly the doll.

Mollie herself is just the same, only she never plays now, but reads and sews when she is not working. The keeper often sits by my house. His hair is white now, like the grandfather's, and he does not dig so many holes in the ground. He sometimes puts his hand on my head, and says, "We are getting to be old folks, you and I, Fritz; we are only good to sit in the sunshine."

This brings me to the most wonderful part of my story, and that is why I left it to the end.

One day a very tall man came to see the keeper. He had very bright eyes, and a kind voice, and he asked the keeper about an old man who had been buried at St. Angelo. They brought out a great book and looked in it a long time, and at last the man said,

"That is he; that is my grandfather's name."

When I heard them speak of the grandfather I
came close to them and looked at the man, but it was
not any one whom I knew.

"This is his dog," said the keeper; "he followed
him to his grave, and almost died of grief, but my
little Mollie saved him."

"That," said the man, "that is my old friend,
Captain Fritz. I have seen his master painting out
that curious black spot on his back; but how ever
did my grandfather come to own him!"

The man has been here very often since then.
He says he is Carl, and sometimes I believe it is
true; but I do not quite know.

I have found out that Mollie likes him; I can tell
it by her eyes and by her voice, and since he came,
she calls me by my old name, Captain Fritz, because
he does. Sometimes when Mollie sews upon the
porch, he sits by me on the grass, and says,

"You are almost at the end, my friend. Now
I wish you could tell me all about yourself before you
go, and about the dear old man we both loved."

When he reads this book he will know it all.

This is the end.

CAPT. FRITZ, HIS FRIENDS AND ADVENTURES.

By EMILY HUNTINGTON MILLER.

Square 12mo, with 70 illustrations $1.50

CAPTAIN FRITZ was a performing dog, and the story of his adventures cannot fail to interest all, old and young. It is one of the brightest books that has been published, and fully sustains Mrs. Miller's reputation as one of the best writers in the country for children.

E. P. DUTTON AND COMPANY, Publishers, New York.

PUSSY TIP-TOES' FAMILY.
A STORY FOR OUR LITTLE GIRLS AND BOYS.
By MRS. D. P. SANFORD.

Ninth Thousand. 1 vol., 4to, with 32 full-page illustrations, boards, with illuminated cover, $1.25 ; elegant cloth, gilt edge, $2.25

THIS beautiful book, the first volume of the series which bears its name, has already found its way into the homes of children all over this country, and its title is as familiar as a household word to over thirty thousand little readers.

E. P. DUTTON AND COMPANY, Publishers, New York.

FRISK AND HIS FLOCK.

BY MRS. D. P. SANFORD.

Eighth Thousand.   1 vol., 4to, with 32 full-page illustrations, boards, with illuminated cover, $1.25 ; elegant cloth, gilt edge, $2.25

"FRISK" is the dog whose picture you will find above, and the boys and girls in the school kept by his mistress were "His Flock," when they were out at play. Children cannot fail to enjoy the story and the large pictures.

E. P. DUTTON AND COMPANY, Publishers, New York.

A HOUSEFUL OF CHILDREN.

BY MRS. D. P. SANFORD.

Sixth Thousand.   1 vol., 4to, profusely illustrated, elegant cloth, gilt edge, $2.25

Calling the Children.

THE third of the Pussy Tip-Toes Series, this volume deals with many of the same characters that have already appeared in "Frisk." The story is always lively and entertaining, and the interest is maintained through the whole book.

E. P. DUTTON AND COMPANY, Publishers, New York.

THE LITTLE BROWN HOUSE
AND THE
CHILDREN WHO LIVED IN IT.

By MRS. D. P. SANFORD.

1 vol., 4to, with 85 illustrations . . . . *Cloth, full gilt, $2.25*

MRS. SANFORD has the happy faculty of interesting children ; and this, the fourth of her large and elegant books, will be likely to prove more attractive than any of the previous ones, on account of the great number of small pictures scattered through its pages, in addition to the many large full-page illustrations.

E. P. DUTTON AND COMPANY, Publishers, New York.

THE CHILDREN'S BIBLE STORY BOOK.

WITH THIRTY-TWO ILLUSTRATIONS.

1 vol., square 16mo, cloth, plain, $1.50 ; cloth, full gilt, $2.00.

THIS volume contains stories from both the Old and New Testaments. Told in simple language, and with a large number of illustrations, they make a book both profitable and interesting to children.

E. P. DUTTON AND COMPANY, Publishers, New York.

THE SUNDAY EVENING HOUR.

By MRS. D. P. SANFORD.

Square 16mo, 304 pages, with 68 illustrations; cloth, plain, $1.50; cloth, gilt, $2.00.

THIS book is for the "many little people who find it hard to occupy themselves quietly and pleasantly through all the hours after church on Sunday;" and parents as well as children, will be thankful to Mrs. Sanford for supplying the long felt need.

E. P. DUTTON AND COMPANY, Publishers, New York.

THE ROSE DALE BOOKS.
EASY READING FOR THE DEAR LITTLE ONES.
By MRS. D. P. SANFORD.

3 vols., square 16mo, each $1.00.   The set, in box, $3.00

ROSE, TOM, AND NED.   IDA AND BABY BELL.
FIVE HAPPY CHILDREN.

For the amusement of the youngest children these three books are unequalled. Printed in type of extra large size, and profusely illustrated, they are the best books to be found for little ones learning to read. The stories are very interestingly told, and the same children appear in all the volumes.

E. P. DUTTON AND COMPANY, Publishers, New York.

www.ingramcontent.com/pod-product-compliance
Lightning Source LLC
Chambersburg PA
CBHW031107020726
47495CB00007B/2087